D1409905

The Moon Scroll

A Magical World Awaits You
Read

THE SECRETS OF DROON

The Moon Scroll

by Tony Abbott

Illustrated by Tim Jessell

A
LITTLE APPLE
PAPERBACK

SCHOLASTIC INC.
New York Toronto London Auckland Sydney
Mexico City New Delhi Hong Kong Buenos Aires

For more information about the continuing saga of Droon,
please visit Tony Abbott's website at
www.tonyabbottbooks.com.

Book design by Dawn Adelman

ISBN-13: 978-0-439-30608-9
ISBN-10: 0-439-30608-6

24 23 22 21 20 19 18 17 16 15 14   9 10 11 12/0

Printed in the U.S.A.   40
First Scholastic printing, May 2002

For my mother,
whose light has always
brightened the shadows

Contents

One

Pictures and Words

"And here's you, the first time you smiled!"

Eric Hinkle was squeezed tight between his parents on his living room couch, looking at pictures. Pictures of himself. As a baby.

"Such a cute smile," said his mother.

"Mom, please," he said.

Eric wasn't exactly smiling now. He was

trying to understand something that happened the last time he was in Droon.

Droon was the secret world he and his friends Julie and Neal had discovered one day beneath his basement.

It was a land of wondrous magic, a realm of danger and mystery and excitement. Together, the three friends had gone there many times.

But on their last adventure, Lord Sparr, the wickedest sorcerer in all of Droon, had told Galen Longbeard, the greatest wizard who ever lived, that Eric was . . . "one of us."

One of . . . *us*!

Galen, Eric, and *Sparr*!

"What does it mean to be one of . . . *us*?" Eric mumbled under his breath.

"It means you've got the Hinkle nose!" said his father, pointing to a picture of Eric at six months old, his tiny face dripping with drool.

"Such a cute nose," said his mother.

Eric laughed. After all, it was true. He did have the family nose. He was certainly a Hinkle.

But he was something else, too. He had been something else for several weeks. Something even his parents didn't know about.

Eric was a wizard.

Yes, a wizard! With powers!

Ever since he was struck by a blast of magic from Princess Keeah — one of his best Droon friends — Eric had been able to do things. He could move stuff just by pointing at it. He could shoot blue light from his fingers. He could even send thoughts into his friends' minds.

But even though his powers made him different, Eric, Julie, and Neal were closer than ever.

He smiled when he thought about how

much fun they had in Droon. Galen had even said that their adventures together were just beginning.

This was a good thing, especially since Galen was off chasing Sparr through the ancient evil underworld known as Goll. Now Keeah would need the three of them more than ever.

The bad part was that they could only get back to Droon if they dreamed about it or if Keeah sent them a secret backward message. And so far, there were no dreams and no messages.

Mr. Hinkle jumped up suddenly. "Forget this little photo album . . ."

"Great," said Eric. "Can I go now — ?"

"Let's get the big album!" his father finished.

"What?" said Eric. "More pictures?"

"More cuteness!" said Mrs. Hinkle delightedly. "Eric, don't you dare run away."

Mr. and Mrs. Hinkle rushed from the room.

Eric sighed. "I'm trapped now . . . unless . . ."

He wondered whether he could speak silent thoughts to his friends from a distance.

Julie, Neal, if you can hear me, come over now.

Just then — *dingdong!* — the doorbell rang.

"Whoa," said Eric, bouncing happily up from the couch. "It worked. I love these powers. No more baby pictures. I did it. I really did it!"

Eric ran through the kitchen to the side door. But even before he could turn the knob, the door burst open and Julie stomped in.

She was nearly in tears.

"What's wrong?" asked Eric.

"Let's go to you-know-where right now," Julie said. "Come on. Let's go —"

"Did you have a dream?" Eric asked.

Julie flicked away a tear. "A nightmare," she said. "Only not about Droon. Look!"

She pulled Eric out the door and pointed across the street to her house. A man was on her front lawn pounding a sign into the ground.

In bright red letters, the sign read:

FOR SALE

Eric was stunned. "Wait, you're . . . *moving?*"

"My dad got a new job," said Julie, a tear rolling down her cheek. "He starts next week. We have to move closer to it."

"But . . . but . . . Julie . . . you . . . can't!" Eric protested. "You and Neal are my best friends. You know the real me! And Galen said our adventures were just beginning. You can't go away!"

Bang-bang-bang. The man finished pounding the sign into the ground.

Julie turned away. "Tell that to him."

"This is crazy," said Eric. "There must be some magic to make this go away."

"It would have to be super magic to change things now. I mean, my dad got a new job!"

Eric nodded. "Keeah will know what to do. I'll call Neal. We can't go to Droon until Keeah sends for us, and we need to be all together."

"Together for maybe the last time," said Julie. She slumped into the kitchen and sat down.

"Don't say that," said Eric. "We'll find a way."

But really, Eric had no clue what that way was. He hoped Keeah could whip up some magic to keep Julie here. Whatever it took, they had to do it.

Just as he reached for the phone, Neal came bounding through the back door.

"Eric, I heard your voice in my head and came right over," said Neal. "I was in my room reading a magazine about this mummy they found in a crusty old tomb in a big old box. Mummies are so cool. Except I'd probably sneeze all over them because of the dust and . . . hey, why are you guys so bummed out? Is it because of the mummy?"

Julie shook her head. "No, it's because of the two little words on the sign in my front yard."

Neal stepped to the door and looked out. He blinked, then he frowned. "By two little words, do you mean . . . *Ylkciuq Emoc*?"

"What?" said Julie. She jumped over to the doorway and stared at the sign in her yard.

"Oh, my gosh!" she gasped. "Eric! Look!"

The three friends piled out the door and stared at the FOR SALE sign. Only the sign no longer said FOR SALE. The letters had changed their shapes.

They now spelled out two other words.

"*Ylkciuq Emoc*," said Eric. "That's backward. Holy cow, it's a backward message from Keeah!"

Neal rubbed his forehead. "Let me see . . . *Ylkciuq Emoc* . . . means . . . uh . . . come quickly!"

"Oh, my gosh!" said Julie. "Maybe Keeah heard about me moving away."

"You're moving away?" said Neal. "Oh, man. Why am I always the last to know? Julie, you've got to stay. Maybe Keeah can help —"

"My idea exactly," said Eric.

"So let's get to Droon now!" said Julie.

They jumped back into the house just as Eric's parents walked into the kitchen.

"Julie, we just saw the FOR SALE sign," said Mrs. Hinkle. "We think of you as one of the family. We didn't know you were moving."

"She won't if we can help it," said Eric. "And we'll be working on our plan, um . . . downstairs, in the basement. See you later, okay —"

"But I found videos of you being born," said Mr. Hinkle. He held up a box and blew a puff of dust off of it. "I was going to make popcorn."

Neal froze. "Popcorn? With salt? And butter?"

"Neal," said Julie. "The basement? Our plan? Remember?"

"Oh, right," said Neal. "The plan. Sorry Mr. H. But you could save some popcorn for me —"

Eric and Julie flung open the basement door and pulled Neal in with them.

"See you later, Mom and Dad!" Eric said.

The three friends jumped downstairs. Instantly, they began dragging cartons away from a small closet under the basement stairs.

"Don't worry, Julie," said Eric when the door was clear. "We'll find a way for you to stay."

"And Keeah will help," Neal added. "I'm sure we can do it, if we put our heads together."

Julie looked at her friends. She dried her eyes and smiled. "What would I do without you guys?"

"Let's hope we never find out," said Eric. He opened the small door and everyone piled in.

"Are we ready?" he asked.

Julie nodded. "I sure am."

Neal grinned. "Let me think. Keeah

needs us. We need Keeah. What are we waiting for?"

Laughing, Eric shut the closet door and switched off the light dangling from the ceiling.

Instantly, the room went dark.

A moment later — *whoosh!* — the gray cement floor vanished. In its place was the top step of a shimmering rainbow staircase.

The staircase curved down and away from Eric's basement and into the land of Droon.

"It's so beautiful," whispered Julie. "I hope I can always come back —"

"You will," said Eric firmly. "I promise."

As they descended, a cool breeze coiled up the stairs. The sun was nearly gone. The air over Droon was turning purple, and the first stars were beginning to dot the sky around them.

Neal tapped Eric's shoulder. "I see something down below. Cliffs and rocks and stuff."

"They're called mountains," said Julie.

A range of low, jagged mountains zigzagged below the curving stairs. Between the two highest peaks a narrow pass snaked through the hills like a road.

"I don't see anyone yet," said Eric, trying to peer into the pass. "Let's keep going."

A blast of chill air swept up from the hills.

Then, just as they neared the bottom of the stairs — *thwang!* — a flaming arrow struck the railing next to Eric's shoulder.

"Ambush!" cried Neal.

"I see chubby red cheeks and shiny black armor," said Eric. "That means — Ninns!"

"Back up the stairs!" said Julie.

"We can't go back," said Neal. "The stairs are fading! Prepare to fall — ahhh!"

The staircase faded, and the children

tumbled and slid and rolled down the slop-
ing hills to the bottom of the pass.

"There they are!" one of the Ninns
yelled.

Instantly, the red-faced warriors loaded
more flaming arrows into their bows.

They took aim at the children.

And they fired.

Thwang-thwang-thwang!

Two

Out of the Mouths of Lizards

"Everybody down!" cried Eric.

The kids flattened to the ground as —
plank! plonk! plunk! — the arrows whizzed
past them and struck the rocky walls behind their heads.

"Spah!" said Neal. "I think I just ate
dirt!"

"Would you rather be target practice for
Ninns?" asked Julie, scrambling into the
shadows.

Plonk! Another arrow struck the ground near Eric. "I don't think they're practicing!"

He scanned for a place to hide, but the cliffs rose too steeply on both sides of the pass.

There was nowhere to go.

"How about flicking your fingers at them," said Neal. "Use your powers —"

Giving a terrible shout, the Ninns charged.

Eric aimed his fingers and spoke a word he had learned. *"Septum . . . conda . . . ro!"*

Zzzz! A beam of blue light shot from his fingertips. But the Ninns were ready. They huddled together and raised their shiny shields.

Zzz-zzz-bloing! The blast of light struck the shields, bounced off, and shot back at the kids.

Blam! The rocks above them exploded into a shower of pebbles and stone dust.

"That didn't work!" said Neal. "A-a-a-choo!"

The Ninns laughed nastily, then loaded their bows, and took aim once more. But before they could shoot their arrows, the pass echoed with the sound of galloping hooves.

Wumpeta-wumpeta!

"It sounds like pilkas," said Julie. "I hope!"

Startled, the Ninns swung around. From the far end of the pass came a man riding a shaggy, six-legged pilka. He held a flaming torch that cast wild shadows on the cliffs.

The man wore a helmet topped with horns.

"It's Keeah's father, King Zello!" shouted Eric.

The king of Droon charged at full speed. In his free hand, he swung a mighty wooden club.

"Yee-haw!" the king cried out. "Out of my way, you nasty Ninns!"

Behind him raced two more pilkas. On the first was the radiant and powerful Relna, Queen of Droon. On the second was Princess Keeah herself, her golden hair flying back in the wind.

The three pilkas burst right through the squad of Ninns and galloped straight for the kids.

"Grab on!" Keeah yelled.

As the three riders swept by, the children leaped up onto the backs of their pilkas.

"Just like a rodeo!" said Eric as he swung up behind King Zello. "Ya-hoo!"

The trio of riders thundered to the end of the pass, then turned their pilkas around swiftly.

"Now, we fight!" said Relna.

"Us, too?" asked Neal. "But I haven't eaten —"

"No, you have a more important task!" said King Zello. "Besides, I need the exercise!"

Laughing, the king jumped from his saddle and launched into battle with the Ninns.

Wump! Whack! Zello swung his club around in a complete circle, and half a dozen Ninns staggered back, tumbling over one another.

"Sparr sent us to hunt the children!" one Ninn shouted. "You can't stop us —"

"We can try!" said the queen as she leveled a stream of blue light at him and his squad of Ninns. They went flying into a heap.

Turning to Keeah, the queen said, "Now go. Your father and I will hold the pass as long as we can. Sparr has sent armies of

Ninns across Droon to find you. So you haven't much time!"

"Ninns are looking for us?" said Julie. "But we just got here. What have we done?"

"It's what Sparr thinks you're going to do that he doesn't like," said Keeah, a smile on her lips. "Now, come on!"

Eric and Neal jumped off of the king's and queen's pilkas, and leaped onto the back of Keeah's pilka with Julie. They rode like the wind through the pass.

"Max is meeting us nearby," Keeah said, spurring her pilka swiftly onward until the sounds of fighting died away. "He has a message from the Guardians."

"The Guardians from the flying city?" said Julie. "I remember them. They're nice. They keep watch over the Tower of Memory."

Everyone remembered them. Especially Eric.

He had one of the strangest experiences of his life in the Guardians' Tower of Memory.

"Galen wants us to find something called the Moon Scroll," said Keeah. "Only the Guardians know what the Scroll is and where it's hidden."

At the sight of a flickering torch ahead, the princess slowed her pilka. Moments later, Max, the friendly eight-legged spider troll, dangled down from the rocks by a silken thread.

"Welcome, children!" he chittered, his voice quivering with excitement and fear. "I heard the fighting. Are you all right?"

"For the moment," said Keeah. She jumped down from her saddle. "Do you have the box?"

Max nodded. He looked both ways, then pulled a small silver chest from a pouch on his waist. He opened it carefully.

Looking inside, the children gasped.

In the chest were two miniature creatures. They looked like lizards, standing on their hind legs and wearing shiny green robes. One of them wore a tiny pair of wire-rimmed glasses.

They were bathed in a bright green glow.

"The Guardians!" said Neal. "Bodo and Vasa! How did you get so . . . small?"

"Do not be alarmed," said Bodo, adjusting his spectacles. "We are actually far from here in our flying city, guarding the Tower of Memory. These are merely images of ourselves —"

"Never mind us," Vasa interrupted. "Listen closely. You know that Galen has followed Lord Sparr into the depths of Goll.

He is trying to foil the sorcerer's latest dark and secret plan."

Bodo nodded. "But you must help, too. The wizard has asked that you find the Moon Scroll."

"We're not really sure what it is," said Keeah.

"The Scroll," said Vasa, "is Galen's poem of early Droon, and one of its oldest histories. The Scroll is extremely valuable. In it, you will learn many secrets about Droon's past."

"Sounds mysterious," said Julie.

Droon's past was full of mysteries and secrets.

Eric recalled how he was trapped in the Tower of Memory once and saw Sparr reading the history of Droon engraved on the Tower's walls.

It was then that Sparr did the weirdest thing.

He began to cry.

Eric could still hear the hissing sound of the sorcerer's tears striking the floor.

"Are you saying that Sparr wants the Moon Scroll, too?" asked Eric.

"Not the Scroll itself," said Bodo, "but what the Scroll will lead you to. It leads to —"

"The wand of Urik," said Vasa.

"I was about to tell them!" said Bodo, frowning over his spectacles at his fellow Guardian. "Urik's wand is an object known to possess deep and wonderful magic for good. Galen believes only the wand will stop Sparr from achieving his dark goals."

"It can create wonders from nothing at all," said Vasa. "It contains more powerful magic than most wizards can do themselves."

"*More* powerful?" said Julie, glancing at Eric.

They were thinking the same thing.

Could this wand keep Julie from moving?

"Alas," Vasa went on. "Sparr has sent many of his Ninns to find Urik's wand first."

"So that's why they ambushed us in the pass," said Julie. "Do they know where the wand is?"

The Guardians shook their heads.

"It was hidden long ago by the earthquakes that destroyed Goll," said Bodo. "The only true way is to follow Galen's poem. But you must hurry. Find the Scroll and you'll find the wand. Find the wand and you'll help save Droon!"

"But where do we start?" asked Julie.

Vasa grinned. "We have told only one person where the Scroll is. He will come when we have gone!"

Then the two tiny figures nodded to each other, and their green glow brightened until it hurt the children's eyes to look at them.

The next moment — *fzzz!* — the images faded.

The Guardians were gone.

The children stood alone in the darkness.

"Um, okay," said Neal. "So where is the person who knows where we're going?"

At that moment, Leep, Galen's prize pilka, galloped into the pass and screeched to a stop right before the children.

Sitting backward in the saddle was a bearded wizard in a long blue robe and tall cone hat. He looked exactly like . . . Galen!

Hopping down and sticking out his foot, he announced, "Good morning! Galen am I."

Everyone laughed. It was not morning.

And the wizard was not Galen.

He was the double Galen created to

take his place while he was away. The only problem was that this wizard did and said everything wrong.

Neal shook his head. "It doesn't seem right to call you Galen. Maybe we should call you Nelag. That's Galen spelled backward."

The pretend wizard bowed. "Nelag. I like it!"

"Good," said Keeah. "Nelag, our mission is to find the Moon Scroll. Where is it hidden?"

"Not far," said Nelag. "In the East, beyond the Forest of Bells, to the middle of the Saladian Plains, at the Ring of Giants. We shall find it at moonrise, so I suggest we go very slowly. We have plenty of time."

"What?" Keeah blinked. "The Forest of Bells is in the West. The Saladian Plains are hours from here. And it's nearly moonrise already, so we need to go quickly!"

"Isn't that what I said?" said Nelag, tugging his long white beard and winking merrily.

Eric sighed. "Well, this is going to be fun. The only person who knows the way is someone who says everything wrong! I guess we go —"

Thwang! An arrow clattered on the stones.

"And we need to go now!" said Keeah.

A band of Ninns charged noisily through the shadows. "Stop the children!" they chanted.

"Okay, we'll stop," said Nelag.

"Which means — let's ride!" cried Neal.

With that, they all leaped onto the pilkas and raced away from the red warriors. As they did, the sky above them silvered with the coming of the moon.

Three

The Brightness of Shadows

The small band rode furiously out of the pass and toward the great, looming Forest of Bells.

"The forest gets its name from the purple-and-blue blossoms hanging overhead," said Max. "They are like great chiming bells!"

When they reached the darkness of the trees, the pilkas charged in without stopping. As they raced through, the flowers began to chime.

Plang! Bing! Dong!

"Such pretty music!" said Nelag.

"Yeah, and if the Ninns couldn't track us before, they sure can now!" said Neal, looking nervously behind them. "Let's hurry out of here."

Amid the chiming and bonging of the bells, the small band broke out the far side of the woods and onto the great flat Saladian Plains.

The plains stretched for miles under the darkening sky.

"The moon will rise very soon," said Keeah, casting looks all around. "But so far, I don't see anything — wait a second, what's that?"

Everyone looked to where she was pointing.

A group of large objects loomed in the distance, blacker than the black night itself.

"The Square of Dwarfs," said Nelag.

"I think he means the Ring of Giants," said Keeah. "It looks like a circle of stones. That's where we'll find the Scroll!"

The pilkas tore across the waving grass to the very center of the plains, then padded softly up to where twenty-four giant blocks of stone stood upright in a circle.

So awesome, Eric thought.

Sliding to the ground, the children stepped into the ring of stones. As soon as they entered the circle, all noise seemed to stop.

The night air grew hushed.

The only sound was their own breathing.

"What *is* this place?" whispered Julie.

"Ticktock, it's a clock!" said Nelag.

Neal looked at him. "Uh-huh, right."

In the center of the circle sat a flat, round stone ten feet across. This stone was colored a deep, rich blue. In the exact middle of it sat a smaller stone bearing a strange symbol.

"Oh, my," chirped Max. "I've seen that mark before. That is my master's name in the old language! Galen was here long ago. We must be close to the Moon Scroll itself!"

Keeah turned to Nelag. "Well, we're in the Ring of Giants. Where will we find the Scroll?"

"It will find you," said Nelag. "I said the Ring was a clock. It's not time yet. I suggest we wait."

They did wait, sitting together on the large blue stone at the center of the Ring, but watching the distance for signs of approaching Ninns.

Night breezes began to waft across the plain.

"Does everyone remember what Galen said of the Scroll?" said Max, peering out into the forest. "He told us the Scroll would explain everything. He said now, more than ever, we need to know the truth. That's what he said."

Eric remembered Galen saying that.

But if the Scroll was full of truth, would it also tell them why Sparr called Eric one of *us*?

And what about the magic wand that the Scroll would lead them to? If they did find it, could its great power keep Julie from moving?

In the hush of the circle of stones, Eric turned to the princess. "We have some bad news," he said. "Julie's moving away."

Keeah's eyes grew wide. "Is this true?"

Julie nodded sadly. Then she told the princess everything that was happening. How her father had taken a new job. How she was going to have to move away very soon. How she worried that she might not be able to come to Droon again.

"Galen said our adventures were just beginning," said Eric. "But it looks like that's wrong."

"We were hoping you might have some magic to help me," Julie said.

"Yeah," said Neal. "Some really cool spell to zap things back to the way they were."

The three friends looked at Keeah expectantly.

She breathed in deeply. "Magic is . . . it shouldn't be used to make problems just disappear. If you change one thing, something you never thought of might change, too. You can't always control it."

"But what about the wand of Urik?" said Eric. "It's supposed to be pretty powerful, right?"

"No one knows what power it possesses," said Keeah. "Besides, it's easy to get caught up in the power of magic and not think about the trouble you can cause with it. Believe me, I know."

"Is that what Sparr did?" asked Neal. "He got too into the power and turned all evil and stuff? I mean, did he start out a good guy like Galen?"

Or like me? thought Eric. *Am I like Galen? Or am I like Sparr? Could I go bad, too? Is that what Sparr meant?*

"No one really knows how Sparr got to

be the way he is," said Keeah. "His past is hidden in the shadows —"

"Bright shadows!" said Nelag suddenly.

Neal laughed. "Bright shadows? That doesn't make too much sense."

"Wait," said Max. "Nelag's right. Look."

A bright light did appear in the shadows beyond the ring of stones. It looked like a big silver face peeping up over the far horizon.

"The moon!" cried Nelag, jumping with delight. "The moon is rising. Everyone, it's time!"

Then it happened.

A single narrow beam of moonlight pierced between two of the upright stones.

Then — *zing! zing! zing!* — the beam bounced from one stone to another until it struck the very center of the blue disk, and the ancient symbol of Galen's name began to sparkle and glow.

Sproing! The small center stone popped up.

"Oh, my!" gasped Keeah.

Underneath the stone was a narrow leather bag about a foot long. Keeah bent down and pulled it out. Opening the bag, she removed a rolled-up tube of old, yellowing paper.

"The Moon Scroll!" murmured Max. "The words of Galen himself! It has not been read for centuries. Oh, this is so exciting!"

The paper itself was rolled tight around two silver rods. On either end of the rods were large crystals that gleamed brightly in the moonlight.

"It's beautiful!" said Julie.

"So are they!" said Nelag, pointing a crooked finger toward the distant trees. "Such a nice red color, aren't they?" he said.

Max sighed. "Nelag, trees are not red —"

"But Ninns are!" said Galen's double.

An instant later, the air filled with the noisy clanging and bonging of bells, as a squad of sword-toting Ninns burst from the flowery forest and charged toward the stone circle.

"*Akkk!*" cried Neal. "Ninns! Surrounding us! All around! On every side! What do we do?"

"*We* don't do anything," said Keeah, looking down. "The Scroll is doing it for us!"

As the moonlight began to fade, other lights — sudden silver lights — shot out of the Scroll's glittering crystals. They shone down onto the flat blue stone they were all standing on.

And the stone began to turn.

"Whoa, merry-go-round!" said Julie, nearly losing her balance. "Better jump off —"

"No!" said Keeah, grabbing Julie's sleeve. "I think this is our way out of here —"

As the stone turned, it began to rise. In seconds it had floated up above the Ring of Giants.

"Stop the children!" shouted the Ninns.

Amid a shower of flaming arrows, the blue disk floated above the silent plain. It rose toward the forest treetops, skimming the high branches and whooshing past the leaves.

"We're on . . . a flying saucer!" said Neal.

The Ninns collected on the plain below them, shaking their fists — but they were too late.

Clouds drifted over the moon, the Ring of Giants fell dark, and the disk rose higher and higher into the night sky.

Keeah turned to her friends, her face bright with the Scroll's silvery light. "The journey of the Moon Scroll — has begun!"

Four

Words and Pictures

The children huddled together on the floating disk as it swept over the dark earth.

The night air wafted coolly over them.

Max glanced nervously over the side at the ground flashing below, then turned to Keeah. "The Ninns will surely continue the hunt, my princess. My master's Scroll will lead us to the wand of Urik. So let us read. Its words haven't been heard for five centuries!"

Taking a deep breath, Keeah unwound the ancient paper. She squinted, then blinked, then sighed. "There's a reason the words haven't been heard for ages," she said. "Galen wrote it backward. It will take me forever to read this!"

"But we don't have forever," said Julie.

"I can probably read some," said Neal, "but it takes time to turn everything backward —"

Neal stopped. He looked at Nelag.

Everyone looked at Nelag. The fake wizard was facing away from them. His shoes were on his hands, and his hat was on his feet.

"Mr. Backward," said Eric. "Um . . . Nelag?"

The wizard turned. "You called?"

Keeah handed Nelag the Scroll. "Can you read this?" she asked.

Nelag glanced at the writing on the

Scroll. He tugged his beard, scratched his ears, licked his lips, then spoke. "It says:

'*I am Galen! I sing now of my wanderings*
    in the land of Droon —'"

Everyone shivered to hear the words of the old wizard come alive again.

"Keep reading," said Max. "Keep reading!"

The stone disk soared over the dark landscape as Nelag began to read again.

"'*Armed with the powerful wand of Urik,*
I came to battle the Evil One, Emperor Ko.
I sought to revenge his terrible deeds.
But Ko sent three goblins to defeat me —'"

"The wand of Urik," said Neal. "That's what we need to find — whoa — what's happening?"

All at once, the stone dipped toward a range of jagged hills. As it did, the silver light again flashed from the Scroll's crystals. This time it struck the rocks below.

"Oh, my gosh," said Keeah. "Look!"

The Scroll's light shone like a spotlight on a solitary figure, wrapped in a blue cape, his light brown hair whipped by a stormy wind.

"It's a boy," said Julie.

"That boy," chittered Max, "is none other than my master — Galen himself — as a child — oh!"

It was true. The boy was Galen. None could mistake the blue cape and the sharp-eyed look of the boy clambering from rock to rock. And hanging in a golden sheath on his belt was a wand, a big purple flower blossoming at its tip.

Neal gasped, "Urik's wand! Hey, Galen, we need that wand!"

"He cannot hear you," said Nelag. "We are here and now. He is there and then. I shall read more of his early words.

'Legends of Ko's palace led me down the
* Ice Hills*
Where the first goblin sprang upon
* me . . .'"*

Eeerk! Crunch! A sudden, terrible squealing and creaking sound came from the rocks.

Galen whirled around, and there it was.

A goblin, ferocious and terrible to look at.

It had the head of a dragon with large teeth, but the body of a man. It leaped over the rocks and was itself made completely of stone.

"Emperor Ko has sent me!" the creature growled. "Give me the wand!"

The boy stood firm. "I will, if you can tell me where Ko is hiding."

The goblin laughed coldly. "Ko never hides!"

"So you're saying he's in his palace?"

The goblin stepped toward Galen. "Of course! I mean . . . no! Never mind! Just give me the wand!"

"I will," said Galen, pulling the wand from its sheath. "Just repeat after me — stone is good."

The goblin ground its stony jaws together. "Repeat after you!? *Arggh!* Stone is good. . . ."

"Fountain is good," said Galen.

"Fountain is good!" growled the goblin.

"Stone is fountain."

"Stone is fountain — what?"

Too late. A rainbow of light burst from Galen's wand — *zzzzz!* — and stone by stone, the goblin was rearranged into a fancy spouting fountain.

"Ha!" said Galen. "In a day, you'll be

ugly again. But for now — what a lovely fountain!"

"You go, Galen," shouted Eric. "Chalk one up for the kid wizard!"

"It's like we're watching a video of the past," said Neal. "Makes me wish we had popcorn after all."

"Only it's not a video," said Julie. "It's what really happened. And that wand is awesome. It really can change things."

The Scroll's light faded, and the stone disk floated up and away from the rocks.

Nelag continued reading.

"'Seeking Ko's palace, I crossed the plains of Kano,
And battled the second goblin, a fiery one.'"

The stone soared through the dark and dipped next over a patch of black and scorched earth.

"There was a great struggle here," said Max.

The light shone down, and there was Galen at the exact moment a fiery goblin jumped out of the earth below. It bore a dragon's head like the first but had red-hot flames leaping off him.

"Give me the wand!" the goblin demanded.

"Am I near the palace of Ko?" asked Galen.

"Ha!" said the goblin. "Is the Valley of Pits near here? Of course not! I mean yes! I mean — *arggh!* Just give me the wand! Ko wants it!"

"I'll fight you for it," said Galen. "But first, I must be comfortable. You give off a lot of heat."

Galen took off his blue cape and laid it on the ground before him. "There. Now I'm ready."

"Ready to perish!" growled the flame goblin.

But the instant the goblin leaped at him, Galen aimed the wand at his cape, saying, "Cape is blue. Water is blue. Cape is water!"

Zzzzz! When the goblin's feet touched the cape, the cape became a swirling pool of water.

"Arggh!" The goblin sank into the water like a stone and — *tssss!* — vanished away to nothing.

"That's one way to cool your fire!" said Galen.

Zzzzz! The water turned back into a blue cape.

"Yes!" shouted Eric. "Galen is amazing!"

The Scroll's light went hazy, the scene dimmed, and the stone disk moved on. Once more, it swept across the dark surface of Droon.

"The stone is taking us far across

Droon," said Keeah, scanning the land rushing by below.

"We must be following Galen's journey to Ko's palace," said Max. "Go on, Nelag, read us more!"

The pretend wizard squinted again at the Scroll.

"'*Before the Valley of Pits lay Grimpen Marsh,*
Where the third goblin was, the worst of the three.
A thing of shadows, he was, a spirit of darkness!'"

The Scroll's light shone on a vast marsh of black water, tangled grass, and thorny reeds.

And there was Galen, sloshing knee-deep in the muck, his wand flickering among the reeds.

"The Valley of Pits is near!" Galen shouted. "I can smell it already! I will find you, Ko, Emperor of Evil! And make you pay for what you did!"

Keeah glanced at Nelag. "What did Ko do?"

Nelag shrugged. "It does not say. Watch!"

Suddenly, there was a splash in the marsh, and it seemed as if the air blurred for a second.

And there they were — fingers flying out of the darkness. Black fingers. In a flash, they plucked Urik's wand right from Galen's hand.

"No!" cried the wizard. He struck back and the wand fell into the marsh with a splash.

As they struggled for it, Galen tore off his cape and tossed it over the goblin.

"I can see you now, fiend!" the wizard cried.

The goblin's form was suddenly visible, but it twisted sharply, flinging the wizard into the water. Spinning around Galen with lightning speed, the goblin wove a chain of marsh grass and spiky reeds around him.

"Let him go!" shouted Eric.

Suddenly, a short, plump man leaped in from nowhere. "I'll help you, young wizard!" he squeaked. Then, snapping his fingers, the little man made the air explode like fireworks in the goblin's face.

Pop! The goblin backed away, howling.

"Ha-ha!" the man twittered. "Don't like light, do you, you ugly thing? Here's more —"

Pop-pop-pop! The goblin sloshed off through the reeds, struggling to tear Galen's cape off, but the little man leaped onto his back.

"Friend! Wait!" called Galen. But the little man and the goblin disappeared into the darkness. Straining to free himself from his prison of grass and reeds, Galen snapped his fingers.

Pop! The air lit up suddenly and his bonds fell away. Galen jumped up laughing.

"Quite a neat trick, after all," he said, snapping his fingers several times and making the air pop with little explosions of light.

"Galen taught me that trick," said Keeah.

"Now, come to me, Wand," said the wizard. "Let us be on our way." But the wand did not come. As Galen searched the marsh around him, he realized that Urik's wand was not there.

"Ko's goblin has stolen it! No!"

Galen fell to his knees and cried out in the night. Then the light faded, and he faded, and the marsh below them was as empty as before.

"Poor Galen," said Max. "To lose the precious wand! Nelag, what happened next?"

"'I never held Urik's wand in my hand again.
But whoever reads these words, know this —
The wand will save Droon, but only if it is found.'"

The friends were silent for a long time.

Finally, Max spoke. "This Moon Scroll, these ancient words of my master Galen, have made the past of Droon come alive. We've seen things from hundreds of years ago — as if they were happening now! Such a story it is . . ."

Keeah put her arm around Max. "But now we must look to the future," she said. "If the goblin stole the wand for Ko, it will be in Ko's palace."

"And Galen said that's in the Valley of Pits," added Neal.

Boing-boing-boing!

"What was that?" said Julie. She leaned over the side of the stone and suddenly jerked back.

There was a face coming up at her. A red face.

"Ninns!" she cried. "Don't they ever give up?"

"Not if your boss is Lord Sparr!" said Neal.

Boing-boing-boing! Some Ninns were lying on their backs while others were jumping on their stomachs, bouncing up higher and higher.

Suddenly — *thwap!* — one Ninn managed to grab the stone, wrapping his claws over the side.

"Is there room for me?" he grunted.

"Sorry, we're full!" cried Max. Together,

the kids peeled the Ninn's claws off, finger by finger. All six of them.

"Not nice!" the warrior howled as he plummeted back onto the pile of his chubby friends.

"Go, stone, go!" said Keeah. "Lead us to the wand!" The flying disk lifted away from the vast marsh, and soared high over the dark earth once more.

Five

Under the Big Turban

It was nearly morning when the floating stone began to drift lower. The marsh
lay far behind them. Now the sun peeked
over the horizon of a vast and empty
desert.

"The Valley of Pits is in the desert?"
asked Julie.

Without warning, the disk settled softly
at the top of a ridge of sandy hills.

"Is this the end of the road?" asked Neal. "I mean flight?"

"I've never been in this part of Droon before," said Max as the six friends hopped off the stone and onto the soft warm sand.

"Galen said Ko had a big palace," said Keeah, looking around. "It should be easy to find. From higher ground we'll be able to see pretty far."

She trudged to the crest of a tall sand dune and looked around. "Oh, no . . ." she said.

"What is it?" said Eric, running to join her.

"The Valley of Pits," she said. "But we're too late . . . too late!"

Below them stood a great valley. The sides were rugged brown rock, leading steeply into a basin that seemed to spread for miles across the flat desert floor.

And all across the valley were pits.

Big black holes had been dug into the brown earth. Some were deep shafts, others were wide gouges cut into the rocky ground.

"I bet treasure hunters did this," said Neal. "I learned about this kind of thing from the mummy magazine. People know there's a hidden palace or tomb. They dig up everything to find it."

Eric shook his head. "Treasure hunters have sure been here. The whole valley is dug up."

"What if someone found the palace of Ko?" said Julie. "What if Sparr already has the wand —"

"Ah, the Valley of Pits, how lovely," said Nelag suddenly. "How happy and peaceful!"

The kids turned. Nelag was staring into

another, smaller valley on the other side of the dune.

Neal snorted a laugh. "No, Nelag, the Valley of Pits is this way. And we're too late."

"I see pits here, too!" said Nelag. "A whole valley of them. Mmmm. Makes me hungry."

Eric followed the pretend wizard's gaze. "A valley of pits? Where do you see . . . whoa!"

In the smaller valley was a cluster of palm trees waving in the desert breeze. Fluttering about them were several large green birds.

One of the birds swooped into a palm tree, then flew out again, with a juicy brown date in its beak. When it had finished eating, it dropped the date's black pit into a pile not far away.

The other birds did the same thing.

The date pits, dropped by many birds for many years, had spilled out across the valley.

Keeah jumped. "Nelag, you found it! The first valley must be there to trick people. This is the real Valley of Pits! We aren't too late to find the wand!"

Without another word, the six friends slid, ran, and tumbled down to the valley below.

The earth was brown with a mixture of dry rock and fine sand as far as they could see.

They made their way to the cluster of palm trees and stood before the largest pile of pits.

Julie made a face. "Such slimy pits. Could the lost palace of Ko really be under here? Eww —"

"Often, things worth the most are hidden by things worth the least!"

Nelag chuckled. "That's silly. Did I say that?"

"No," said a strange voice. "I did!"

The kids wheeled around.

Sitting cross-legged on top of a nearby rock was a bearded man dressed in flowing white robes; he wore an enormous blue turban, at least three feet across. The turban cast a shadow that covered him entirely. "Hoja!" he said to them.

"Um, Hoja to you, too," said Keeah.

The old man chuckled merrily. "No, no, I am Hoja! Hoja is my name. What are yours?"

Keeah stepped over and bowed. "I am Keeah. These are my friends." She introduced everyone.

"Pleased to meet you," said the man,

his beard wagging as he spoke. "Welcome to my abode."

Julie looked around. "Abode? Do you live out here all alone? I mean . . . outside?"

Hoja laughed. "Who needs a house who has such a hat as mine? As for being alone, I am not alone. You are here! And where your friends are, so is your home. A wise man told me that once."

"What are you doing in the desert?" asked Max.

"I am a herder of animals," said Hoja. "By the way, you haven't seen my flock, have you?"

"Flock?" said Neal. "You mean like sheep?"

"They're called fluffems," said Hoja. "And they are sort of . . . kind of . . . and they have . . . well, they're fluffy like sheep. But enough about them. You seek the lost palace of Ko, don't you?"

Keeah started. "How did you know that?"

"No one comes to these parts for any other reason," Hoja said. Then he laughed. "Come to think of it, no one comes here for *any* reason!"

Nelag laughed, too. "Well, we have plenty of time to find the palace." Then Nelag promptly fell asleep.

Eric shook his head. "What he means is, a ton of Ninns have been following us."

"Then dig for the palace door right under the mound of date pits," said Hoja. He handed the children dried-out palm leaves for digging.

"Now, you'd better get going. I must wait here until my flock returns."

Neal looked about at the vast desert around them. "How long have they been gone?"

"Oh, let me see . . ." Hoja began. "It's

nearly noon . . . today is . . . oh, about five centuries!"

Eric blinked, wondering just how old the man was. "You've been waiting here that long?"

"No time is long, if you have hope," said Hoja. "The main thing is that you get to work. But remember, once you get inside the palace, you'll be in Goll. It's a bad place, where evil has the upper hand. Best of luck to you and don't forget your sleepy friend!"

Keeah smiled and gently woke Nelag.

"Are we there yet?" the pretend wizard asked.

The children headed for the mound of pits.

"Oh, and Urik, here!" said Hoja. He slung a small sack at Eric. "You'll need some help!"

Eric caught the bag. "Thanks, but my name's Eric — huh?"

When he looked back, the man was gone, turban and all. As if he had never been there.

"Okay, he's strange," mumbled Eric.

"Odd disappearing fellow!" said Max. Then he peered in the sack and frowned. In it were six small candles. "But these candles are mere stubs. They won't last a minute."

"But a minute may last forever," said Nelag.

Neal made a face. "Uh-huh."

"Let's start," said Keeah. "It's nearly noon."

Using their dried palm leaves, the six friends dug as quickly as they could.

They scraped and shoveled and dug at the date pits. An hour passed. Two hours.

When the sun grew its hottest, Max took a small container of water from his pouch and passed it around. Nelag gave

everyone handfuls of curious dried fruit while they worked.

Finally, Keeah's palm leaf struck something hard. It snapped in half. "I found something," she said. "Maybe it's the door to the lost palace!"

"And the way to the wand," said Julie.

More quickly than before, the six of them shoveled away the pits and the sand.

And, suddenly, there it was, glinting under the afternoon sun. A shiny black door.

And in the center was a strange golden design.

A triangle, pointing down, with two horns thrusting up the sides.

"That symbol is here," Nelag said, tapping the unfurled Moon Scroll. "It is the symbol of Ko himself, ancient evil emperor of Goll."

Keeah gasped. "Then we've found it —"

Thwang! A flaming arrow whizzed past her ear.

"And the Ninns found us!" cried Neal. "Let's get in there — now!"

The children pulled open the heavy door and jumped through just as an army of Ninns swarmed over the ridge and into the Valley of Pits.

Six

Lost in the Lost Palace

The friends pushed past the large black door and tumbled into a narrow stone corridor.

"Help me close the door!" urged Max.

Wham-am-am! The slamming of the door echoed around and around in the darkness.

"Scary sound," said Neal. "Plus it's real dark."

Using sparks from their fingertips, Eric

and Keeah lit each of the six small candles Hoja had given them. The flickering light cast strange shadows on the black walls of the passage.

Julie turned and looked at the door. "Wait a second. Did we just trap ourselves in here?"

Eric looked at the door, too. He wished he could make some kind of joke about something. But he couldn't think of anything funny. Entering the ancient palace of the old evil emperor of Goll wasn't a funny thing. It was maybe the scariest thing imaginable.

But it was too late to turn back now.

Eric gulped. "I guess we *are* trapped in here."

"Then there's only one direction to go," said Keeah. "Straight ahead. Let's find the wand."

The corridor slanted down. Slowly, cautiously, they descended into the gloom.

"Today is fun, isn't it?" said Nelag suddenly. "Let's hope yesterday will be even more fun!"

"You mean tomorrow, right?" said Neal, taking a careful step. "When we're safe at home?"

"Wherever that home is," added Julie.

Nelag shook his head. "No. I mean *yesterday*. For behold . . . look at our wonderful candles!"

Instead of melting down, the stubby candles Hoja had given them were growing larger and brighter with every step they took.

Max shivered. "Either the candles are magic, or . . . or . . . we are going back through time. We are . . . entering the past!"

A sudden sound of moaning wind came

up — *whoom-oom!* It started loudly from the darkness ahead, rushed over the children, then died out in the corridor behind.

"That wind went right *through* me," said Julie.

"It's warm air," said Keeah.

"Then why am I shivering?" said Neal. "Plus, we're inside here. So where did the wind come from?"

Eric moved up beside Keeah. "There, where the passage narrows. There's an opening."

He stepped forward and the others followed behind. The passage continued to narrow until the walls were only a foot apart.

"This scares me," Max whispered. "I wish my master were here."

"I think we all do," said Keeah. "Eric, can you get to the opening?"

"I think so." Turning sideways to make

himself as flat as possible, Eric edged toward the narrow opening and slid his candle through it. He let his eyes get accustomed to the flickering flame, then he peered in.

Strange shapes began to loom out of the darkness. His pulse started to race. He gasped softly.

"Eric, what do you see?" asked Keeah.

He felt barely able to speak.

"What's in there?" asked Julie, sliding closer.

"Wonderful things!" Eric said finally. "Incredible stuff. Golden pots, swords, jewels, statues!"

Keeah drew a deep breath. "Any wands?"

"No, not yet," he said. "But these stones are loose. I think I can make the opening bigger."

He struck one of the loose stones with his palm. It tumbled into the chamber beyond. Then another went, and another. Soon, the opening was large enough to enter. One by one, the kids slid down a wall of rock to a floor on the other side.

Huddling together and holding their candles high, they found themselves in a large stone chamber. Heavy stone columns held up the distant ceiling. The walls were covered with thick layers of dust.

"This place needs a decorator," said Julie.

"Or a vacuum cleaner," said Neal. "My allergies are going to go nuts in here."

Piled right up to the ceiling were mounds of treasure. Silver daggers, bronze cups, shields, helmets, even a golden chariot. Here and there were stacks of spears, leaning against one another, their tips touching to form a deadly cone.

"Unbelievable riches," said Max. "Ko

was famous for trying to conquer all of Droon."

"Is that where Sparr got the idea?" said Julie.

"The wand should be in plain sight," said Nelag.

Keeah laughed. "You mean it's most likely hidden, perhaps in a secret room."

Neal suddenly clutched his nose. "The dust . . . I can't take the . . . a-choo!" He sneezed in the shadows and blew a huge cloud of dust off the wall nearest him. "Sorry!"

"Don't be," said Keeah. "Look what you did."

Underneath the centuries of dust were . . .

"Pictures," said Keeah. "The walls are covered with them." She brushed her hand on the wall, and an image appeared. It was

a terrible beast with three eyes, black horns, and a pair of curved tusks. Its body was covered with shaggy black hair and it had four thick arms and two tails.

"Is that —" Eric said, his heart pounding.

"Ko," said Nelag, unrolling the Moon Scroll. He read what was written there.

"'By force and fear the beast called Ko
Ruled the wicked empire of Goll.
But Goll was not enough for him.
He wanted all of Droon. And more than
    Droon.'"

"More than Droon?" Julie asked.

"Galen stopped him," said Keeah. "But these paintings show him in his prime."

The walls were covered with pictures of Ko.

Ko in battle.

Ko seated on his throne.

Ko ascending a steep black stairway.

Eric wondered where that stairway led.

Max snorted angrily. "It's Ko, Ko, Ko, and nothing but Ko. He's everywhere you look."

"Not everywhere," said Eric as he blew the dust off a symbol carved into the far wall.

The symbol was similar to Ko's, a triangle with horns. But this one had a lightning bolt right through the face of the triangle.

Nelag peeked over his shoulder. "Perhaps the Scroll says something about this one. . . ."

Eric shone his candle over the carving and ran his fingers over it. But the moment he touched it, he heard a grinding sound, as if stones were moving, one against the other. Suddenly — *vrrrt!* — the stone beneath Eric's feet moved.

"Oh, dear!" said Nelag, jumping back and dropping the Scroll.

Eric tried to leap out of the way but the floor simply collapsed under him.

"Helppppp!" he cried.

But there was nothing anyone could do.

With a yelp and a whooshing sound, Eric fell through the floor and vanished into the darkness below.

Seven

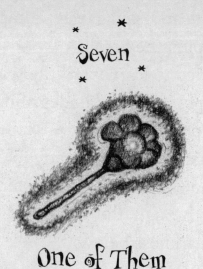

One of Them

Bump! Blam! Bonk! Eric bounced from one stone to another, hurtling down a deep shaft until — "*ooof!* yikes! owww!" — he landed in a heap in a room far below where he started.

The room was pitch black.

"Eric-ic-ic-ic!" a voice echoed down to him.

He moved. His shoulder hurt the most,

but nothing seemed broken. "Can you hear me-e-e?" he called out.

"We'll get you out-out-out!" Neal's voice echoed down the shaft. "Just stay put-ut-ut!"

Eric managed to laugh. "Where would I go?"

While his friends scrambled to find a way down to him, he stood up. But when he took a step, something rolled under his foot, and he crashed to the floor again.

"Enough with the falling," he said, rubbing his shoulder again. Feeling around, his hand grasped what had made him fall. It was round and narrow.

"The Moon Scroll!" he said. He opened the Scroll. Instantly, its light flashed out.

He was in a room, smaller than the first, and different. It was filled with furniture — a golden chair, a jeweled chest, a wardrobe, and a bed covered in tapestries that, though once colorful, were now tattered and faded.

Dust covered everything.

Of course, thought Eric. *The palace has been empty for centuries.*

Like the walls in the upper room, the ones here were covered with pictures, but they were not pictures of Ko. They were of a woman wearing a white robe and a crown of dazzling light.

"She's beautiful. . . ."

Slowly translating Galen's ancient words, Eric read from the Scroll.

"'Let me remember — O terrible night — How Zara, Queen of Light, was stolen by Ko!'"

Eric frowned. "Queen of Light? Stolen?"

When he held the Scroll up to the wall

for light, the woman's eyes seemed to look directly into his.

Zara. There was something musical in the name, something very old about it, but alive and wonderful, too. Next to her picture was her symbol in the ancient Droon language.

It looked like a stinger or a lightning bolt.

"Have I seen this one before?" he mumbled.

A second panel showed the queen, now lying in a bed, her face pale. Behind the bed stood the menacing figure of Ko himself, his eyes cold, his four arms folded. Next to him crouched the three goblins that had fought Galen.

Standing behind them all was that same wide black stairway Eric had noticed from earlier pictures. It led all the way up to the clouds.

He read from the Scroll again.

"'She wasted away, a prisoner in Ko's palace,
And when she died all the wizards wept.'"

Eric was stung by the words. It was so sad. Then he noticed something else. Pictured beside the bed was a boy. He was covering his face, and his tears were running into a blue pool on the floor.

"The wizards wept," Eric said. "But who —"

The Moon Scroll flashed suddenly.

And someone spoke.

"You shouldn't be here."

Eric turned and peered into the gloom. "Guys? Is that you? Are you there?"

"This is my mother's room."

The voice was behind him. It sounded angry.

Eric whirled around, shining the light into every shadow. The room was empty. But when he turned to the painting again, he gasped.

"The boy!"

The boy kneeling by the bed was no longer in the picture. There was the bed, the dying queen, the pool of tears. But no boy.

Eric staggered back. "He's . . . gone —"

"I'm not gone," said the voice.

And the boy stepped out of the shadows and into the silver light of the Scroll.

"Oh, my gosh," muttered Eric.

The boy's face was pale and his eyes were angry. Folded around his shoulders was a cape as slick and glistening as a crow's feathers.

But that wasn't all. Behind each ear was a small pointed fin, like a jagged fish fin.

The fins were dark blue, almost purple.

Eric gasped. "It's . . . you! You're . . . him! I mean . . . Sparr . . . as a kid . . . Kid Sparr!"

It was Sparr. There was no mistake. He walked farther into the ring of light cast by the Scroll. Sparr looked to be the same age as Eric himself. Slowly, he began to circle Eric.

Hold on, Eric, we're coming!

In his mind, Eric heard Keeah's voice, speaking silently from some distant room in the palace. The boy didn't seem to hear. Eric answered.

Sparr is here! he said. *I think the Scroll brought him to life. Sparr . . . as a kid! Hurry!*

Sparr's eyes burned as he continued to circle Eric. "Your face . . ." he said.

"What? What about my face?"

"Are you one of . . . us?"

Eric nearly fainted to hear those words again, this time from Sparr as a boy.

What did he mean?

"I'm not evil, if that's what you mean," said Eric. "*Is* that what you mean?"

Eric, hold tight, we're nearly there! the voice of Keeah sounded in his head. She seemed nearby.

Sparr was silent, and Eric tried to back away farther. As he did, more dust fell from the wall, showing more pictures of the beautiful queen.

"Um, is that your mother in the picture?"

Sparr's eyes flashed red. "Ko stole us from our home. Because of my mother's great power."

"Uh-huh," said Eric, his eyes darting beyond the silver light for a way out. "She seems —"

"She was the Queen of Light!" Sparr snapped. "The greatest wizard ever!"

"But Ko was evil, right?" asked Eric.

The boy glared at Eric. "After my mother was . . . gone, Ko taught me what else my magic could do. Powerful things. Ko made me one of them."

Eric froze. *One of them? Meaning what?*

Sparr touched his fins. "A sorcerer . . ."

All of a sudden — *crash!* — the wall behind Sparr blew open, and Keeah, Julie, Neal, Max, and Nelag tumbled into a heap at the feet of the young sorcerer.

"So you brought your friends along?" Sparr said, glaring at them. "Ko always told me someone would come to steal the wand. You'll never get it." Then he laughed coldly.

"Holy cow, we've heard that laugh before!" said Neal. "I mean, after! I mean — yikes, it's Kid Sparr — let's get out of here!"

"Not before I destroy you!" Sparr snapped.

Kkk-blam! A bolt of red light shot from his fingers, and Max, Nelag, and the kids were hurled back into the wall.

"Two can play that game," said Keeah, jumping to her feet. "Eric, let's blast him —"

Together, the two kids sent a sparkling stream of blue light from their fingertips. The light drifted a few inches in the air, then faded to nothing.

Sparr grinned. "You are in Goll, now," he said. "Wizard powers don't work here. Only those of a sorcerer. Like Ko. And like me. Watch this!"

Sparr aimed his fingers at the wall next to him.

Kkkkk! Another bolt of red light shot straight into the wall at the picture of the three goblins that had battled Galen for the wand.

"Oh, no," chittered Max. "Not them!"

Sparr laughed. "Yes, them! Goblins!

Come, come, my little playmates, let's have some fun!"

With a terrible wrenching, squealing, grinding sound, the three goblins of Ko — the dragon-headed goblins of stone and fire, and the third one, the dark smear of air — peeled themselves off the wall and leaped in front of the children.

"Ko taught me my powers well," said Sparr. "Pretty clever, don't you think?"

"You know what I think is clever?" said Nelag. "Running. Running is clever. I also think that we should be running right now!"

The goblins crouched, ready to leap again.

"Now is good," said Julie.

"I'm for running now, too," said Keeah. Max nodded. "Or how about . . . NOW!"

"Goblins!" Sparr half yelled, half howled. "Chase them — into the playground!"

As the goblins jumped at them, the children, Max, and especially Nelag . . . ran.

Eight

The Goblin Chase

Keeah led everyone back through the hole they had made. They clambered up into one twisting corridor after another, only steps ahead of the goblins.

"Hurry!" cried Neal. "Those uglies are right on my tail! And I don't even have a tail!"

"Hurry where?" said Keeah breathlessly. "I don't know which way I'm going!"

"I do!" said Nelag unexpectedly. "Follow me!" He rushed upward into a maze of hallways and stairways and corridors, then screeched left.

Passages crisscrossed one another confusingly. Walls shot up, others fell away, stairs led coiling upward, ramps snaked back down into the darkness.

"It's a crazy maze!" said Julie. "Sparr must have grown up in this wicked playground!"

Only Nelag seemed to know which way to go. Eric guessed that it was because everything was mixed up for him anyway.

"Turn right!" Galen's double shouted, leaping into one dark corridor. "Now up we go!" he cried, springing up a set of curving steps.

Every time the kids thought they had lost the goblins, Neal sneezed again and there they were.

"You'll never find Urik's wand!" the first said.

"Don't mention the secret room!" said the second. "I mean — there is no secret room! *Arggh!*"

"So helpful, aren't they?" chirped Max.

Nelag zigzagged left, then right, and finally bounded into a small, round room. He stopped.

Everyone stopped. There were eight dark passages leading off the room.

"We're in the center of the maze," said Keeah.

Eric listened but couldn't hear the goblins. "Good work, Nelag, I think we lost them."

"We lost ourselves, too," said Julie. "Anybody have any —"

"Tissues?" said Neal. "Anybody have any tissues? Because I'm going to . . . going to . . . oh, no . . . a-choo!" The sneeze echoed around the small room and out into the passageways.

"I hear them!" shouted the stone goblin from a passage on the right.

"Me, too!" shouted the fire goblin from a passage on the left.

Their feet pounded and stomped as they came rushing from both directions.

"Sorry!" said Neal. "But what do we do now?"

"Quack," said Nelag calmly. "Quack."

Julie blinked. "Quack?" Then she jumped. "I think he means — DUCK!"

Everyone flattened to the floor at the exact moment the stone goblin and the fire goblin rushed in from opposite directions.

"Got you now — um, what?" yelled one.

"Aha! I mean — oh, no!" yelled the other.

There was a great popping sound when the fire goblin and the stone goblin slammed into each other.

The looks on their faces showed shock.

Then the looks on their faces were gone.

And so were they.

POOOOM! And the small room was filled with nothing but smoke and pebbles.

"Yahoo!" cried Eric. "Two down, one to go!"

Then out of the swirling smoke came a rush of air, a smear of darkness. It snuffed the candles. Even the Moon Scroll's crystals dimmed and went out.

"The shadow goblin," said Keeah.

"I don't like him," said Neal. "Let's do that running thing again."

And they did run, straight into the darkest of the dark passages.

"We're going down," said Max, running on the walls. "Into the deepest part of the palace."

But the invisible goblin was right behind them. The children could feel its cold presence gaining ground with each twist of the maze.

They ran. The goblin followed.

They ran faster. It followed faster. Then it thrust out its hands.

"Help!" yelled Julie. "It's . . . got . . . me!"

"Keeah, do the snappy-finger thing!" said Eric.

The princess spun on her heels and snapped her fingers loudly.

Pop! A bright flame flashed in the passage, and the shadow goblin fell back, freeing Julie from its grasp.

"He hates the light!" said Keeah with a smile. "Well, Goblin, take this — and this!"

Pop! Pop! She kept snapping her fingers and the goblin howled and shrieked and fell back into the darkness behind them. The kids heard its footsteps racing back through the maze.

"And once more for good luck!" said Keeah.

Pop . . . The passage lit up for an instant, then plunged back into darkness.

"Now, to find a way out of here," said Max.

"Wait," said Eric suddenly. "Keeah, explode another one of those things."

"But the goblin's gone," she said. "My powers are nearly gone, too. It's Goll, remember, my powers are limited here."

"But I saw something just now," said Eric.

Keeah tried one last time. *P-p-p-pop* . . .

The passage lit up once more, and there it was, a strange carving on the wall by the ceiling.

Julie breathed in suddenly. "Is that —"

Eric nodded. "Urik's wand. I think we found the secret room."

He pressed a stone beneath the carving.

Vrrrt! The wall slid aside.

And they entered the secret room of the wand.

Nine

Tomb of Ko, Tears of Sparr

The secret chamber lay deep in the center of Ko's palace. They could tell because of the smell. It was damp and musty and just plain foul.

"The smell of evil," said Max, holding his nose. Everyone held their noses as they entered.

"There's something creepy about this place," said Neal. "Something very creepy."

Eric made a face. "Yeah, and the very

creepy thing is standing at the far end of the room."

They all looked.

An enormous and strangely shaped box made of black stone stood against the back wall.

Julie shivered. "The shape of this box is the same as, um . . ."

"K-k-ko," Max stuttered. "Th-th-this must be his burial chamber, the t-t-tomb of Ko."

"But that isn't the worst part," said Nelag. He pointed to carvings on the box itself. They showed Ko being put into the black box.

In his hand was the golden wand of Urik.

Neal gulped loudly. "Let me get this straight. You mean . . . the wand that we've been looking for all this time, this great and powerful magic wand, the fabulous wand of Urik, is . . . in there . . . with Ko?"

"Ding-ding-ding! Correct answer!" said Nelag.

"And here's why we need to get it," said Eric, his hands quivering as he pointed to another carving on the box.

It showed the wand of Urik. From the purple flower at one end came a shimmering rainbow of light. And the light itself formed a set of stairs.

A set of rainbow-colored stairs.

Keeah gasped. "The magic staircase? The wand of Urik *created* the magic staircase? Oh, my gosh. It must be the most powerful magical object ever made!"

"That's why we can't let Sparr have it," said Eric. "And that's why we need to open this box now, and then scoot out of here as fast as our legs can carry us. Neal, let's get this lid off before Sparr conjures more goblins to stop us."

Neal shrank back. "Um . . . no."

"But you said mummies were so cool," said Julie. "You wanted to explore tombs. Well . . ."

"Mummies are cool in magazines!" said Neal. "Not in real life. You do it."

Keeah laughed. "Eric, I'll help you. Neal, everybody, watch the door."

While everyone scrambled to the door, Eric and Keeah started pushing at the heavy black lid. It began to move.

"We shouldn't be doing this," Neal mumbled.

They pushed harder.

"He's dead in there, you know," said Neal.

The lid slid a bit, then more. Finally, it moved aside.

Eric closed his eyes. "I can't look! I can't look!"

Keeah made a sudden wincing noise. Then she pounded her fist on the black lid. "It's empty!"

"Empty?" Eric blinked his eyes open. "But . . . but . . . what?"

Max scrambled over from the door. So did Julie and Neal. They peered into the box. There was no Ko. No beautiful magic wand.

The tomb was empty.

Almost.

Eric reached in and pulled out an old, dry stick. "There's just this old thing," he said. The stick began to crumble in his hand. "I can't believe it. Our journey, our whole mission, was to find Urik's wand. But we failed! Galen needs the wand. Instead, there's only this stick! Someone

tricked us. They got here before us and left this . . . joke." Eric threw the stick across the room.

"Trick, stick, Urik, it all rhymes!" said Nelag.

Everyone turned to him. He was leaning against the wall behind them.

"Uh," said Keeah, "who's watching the door?"

Nelag raised his hand. "Only me."

"But you're on the wrong side of the room."

"I can watch the door from here," said Nelag. "I mean, it's very boring watching a door. I've been watching it all this time and it hasn't done a single thing —"

BLAM! The door blasted open and Sparr entered, his fingertips sparking with red light.

"Now it's doing something," said Nelag.

"How dare you enter the tomb of Ko!"

snarled the boy sorcerer. "He was Emperor of Goll. He was —"

"An animal?" Neal snarled angrily. "Sort of like you, Sparr. You're like an animal, too."

"No, he's not," said Julie. "Animals are cute and fluffy. You scratch them behind the ears —"

"Right," said Neal. "Who'd ever scratch *him* behind the ears? I mean . . . eewww!"

Who? Eric knew who. Zara, Queen of Light. She loved Sparr. She was Sparr's mother.

"Ko was like a father to me —" said Sparr.

A father? thought Eric. *What about your mother? She was good. She was the Queen of Light!*

Eric finally realized why Sparr had cried that day in the Tower of Memory. He was remembering his mother. Even grown up,

Sparr still bore the painful memory of the day she left him here alone. The day Zara died and he was left with Ko.

All alone, with no one but evil Ko.

It had all come together for Eric. The wall carvings of the boy at his mother's bedside. The radiant Queen of Light.

The pool of tears.

"Ko told me that others would try to stop my quest," said the boy sorcerer.

"What quest?" asked Keeah. "To rule Droon?"

"For starters," he replied. "And I think I'll start now."

His fingers sparking with red light, Sparr raised his hands.

Blam! A pillar exploded and fell to the floor.

Blam! Another pillar toppled and struck the nearby wall. A glimmer of sunlight burst into the chamber.

Eric moved toward the crack in the wall, but kept staring at the cold, dark eyes of young Sparr, flashing so angrily in the sunlight.

Thinking of the Queen of Light, Eric felt his own eyes sting. He felt tears welling up in them, and his throat getting tight.

But what was the Queen of Light to him?

Zara was just a dusty ancient name and a symbol like a lightning bolt. And yet, Eric knew, to speak her name even once would sting as deeply for him as for Sparr himself.

Why?

What did he and Sparr have in common?

They were like day and night, weren't they?

Weren't they?

Blam! Blam! Another pillar fell and more sunlight slanted through the cracked wall.

The young sorcerer closed in on them, his power seeming to grow with each step he took toward the black stone box of Ko.

But Eric knew he could stop him.

He had to do it.

And he did.

He whispered the name. "Zara!"

The name seemed to echo around the stones.

Sparr stopped moving.

When the word formed on his lips, it hurt Eric deeply, as if a lightning bolt itself had struck him.

But just as Eric staggered, so did Sparr.

The sorcerer fell to his knees, his face in his hands.

Tssss! A tear hissed where it struck the floor. And the floor quaked.

"Let's get out of here!" cried Max. "Now!"

Keeah helped pull Eric out of the chamber as the others pushed their way through the cracked wall and into the shimmering light of day.

And the great lost palace of Ko and all the ghosts in it quaked and quivered and toppled down on itself, buried even deeper under mountains of sand and rock, lost to the past once more.

Ten

The Gift

Gasping for air, the six friends leaped from the crumbling ruins and out into the hot desert sun.

"We're out!" Neal cried, clambering across the sand. "And we're away from that creepy ghost."

They were out. And it felt good to breathe real air again. Fresh, warm desert air, wafting across the rolling hills and dunes of Droon.

"What happened in there?" said Keeah, falling exhausted to the sand.

Eric looked at her. He saw in her face the same wonder and amazement that he felt.

"I'm not sure," he said. "But I think we learned something deep about Lord Sparr, something we didn't know —"

"I know something!" said Nelag suddenly. "The sun is over the hills and so are the Ninns!"

"You've got to be kidding," Julie groaned.

But Nelag wasn't kidding. Hundreds of Ninns were pouring into the valley, turning the hillside red with their bright, crayon-colored skin.

"And I thought we had done all our running for one day!" said Neal. "Come on, everyone, let's make tracks!"

"Wait a moment," said Max. "The Ninns are all pointing at Eric for some reason."

Eric turned. The vast hordes of red warriors were jumping and pointing at him. "Why me?"

"Because they think that stick you've got is the wand," said Keeah.

Eric looked down. Stuck in his sneaker laces was the old stick from Ko's tomb. "I must have dragged this with me on the way out. Too bad it's not Urik's wand. I'd conjure up an army of our own!" Then he flung the stick over his shoulder and yelled to the Ninns, "It's just a stick!"

The Ninns charged, then stopped suddenly in their tracks.

"Why did they do that?" asked Max.

"Because of me!" said a voice behind them.

They turned and saw Hoja, his white robes flying. He was riding up over a dune on the back of an enormous beast. It was nine feet tall, had a woolly pink coat, a long furry trunk, and big feet.

"You see," said Hoja. "I found my fluf-fems!"

He whistled brightly, and the ground thundered as the rest of his flock galloped over the crest of the dune, roaring and snorting loudly.

At the sight of them, the Ninns shrieked. Then they turned and made their own thundering noise, taking flight as quickly as they had come.

"Yahoo!" the children cheered.

Hoja grinned. "Glad to be of service. Now a little something to speed you home."

The little man unwrapped his giant tur-ban and threw out its length of blue cloth. It sparkled in the sunlight. Then, before their eyes it turned into a river, winding across the desert sands.

A small boat was floating lightly by one of its banks.

"By morning, Princess, you will be home, where your parents await your safe return."

"But your turban," said Keeah. "That river . . . it's . . . it's . . ."

"Galen's cape?" said Hoja, his plump cheeks blushing. "Yes. It was I who chased the shadow goblin so many years ago. I am Hoja, Seventh Genie of the Dove. For twelve days and nights, I fought that terrible goblin. He overcame me by trickery, taking Urik's wand into Ko's palace."

"Wicked thief!" said Neal.

"Wicked indeed!" said Hoja. "I have been waiting for five centuries for someone to find the wand. And now you have done it."

The children looked at one another. They realized all over again that they had failed in their mission.

"But we didn't find the wand," said Eric.

"Maybe it's lost forever," said Keeah. "Maybe no one will ever find it. Not even Lord Sparr."

Hoja frowned. "Lost? Oh, dear. Yet, somehow, I am free! Best not to complain. Perhaps it is as a wise man once said. Often, things worth the most are hidden by things worth the least."

Nelag laughed. "But *you* said that."

"Did I?" Hoja said with a chuckle. "Then it's time for me to go think of new things to say! In fact, it's time for everyone to go. Look."

The rainbow stairs shimmered into view over a nearby dune. They seemed to shine more brilliantly than ever before.

"Until next time — good-bye!" said the genie. Then, tugging the reins of his fluffem, he whistled to his flock, and they all thundered off into the distance and vanished into the hazy air.

"Cool dude," said Neal. "And the first genie I ever met. I like him."

"He helped my master," said Max.

"He was Galen's friend," said Keeah, opening the Moon Scroll one more time. "Maybe his first real friend. Listen to this:

'*Alone, I wandered, until I found a friend. Then I knew I had a family. Then I was home.*'"

"Which is where we must all go now," said Max. "Good-bye, children. We'll see you quite soon, I'm sure."

Keeah hugged Julie. "You will come back," she said. "I'll keep working on it."

"Thanks," said Julie.

Finally, Nelag turned to the kids and stuck out his foot. "Hello!" he said. "See you recently!"

Laughing, the three friends started up the

staircase. They turned to wave at Keeah, Max, and Nelag once more before entering a layer of wispy clouds.

As they neared the top, Neal laughed. "Hey, Eric, you're dragging that stick again!"

Eric looked down and saw the broken stick from Ko's tomb tucked into his sneaker again.

"This thing just won't get lost!" he said. "Stick, go home!" With that, he tossed it through the clouds to the desert below.

"Too bad we didn't find the wand," said Julie.

Eric nodded. "I hoped it would help us. But I'm still not going to let you just move away. The three of us, we're too much of a family."

"Us, a family?" Julie looked at Eric. "That's like what Galen said in the Scroll. I guess your friends are sort of your family."

Neal nodded. "Absolutely. Besides, I'd miss you too much if you left. Also your mom's blueberry pancakes. They're awesome."

Julie smiled. "No, you guys are awesome."

She opened the closet door, and they all piled back into Eric's basement.

Later, after Julie and Neal had gone home, Eric went to his room. On his bed, his parents had left the big photo album, open to a page with pictures of him and Julie and Neal.

In one, they were all climbing a tree together. Neal's face was smeared with peanut butter. Julie was crossing her eyes and had leaves stuck in her hair. Eric was hanging upside down from a branch.

They were four years old.

"Oh, man," he said, his eyes stinging as

they had before. He and Julie and Neal had done a lot together. They had known one another forever.

"She can't go away," he said. "She's family. She's one of us. This can't happen. . . ."

He picked up the album and sat down on the bed. "Hey!" He sprang back up again. There was something sharp under his blanket. He rolled it back and there on the bedsheet lay a stick. The same stick he had thrown away three times.

He gasped. "What are *you* doing here? I already threw you away! Three whole times!"

Eric stepped over to his wastebasket. He was about to throw the stick in, when it began to tingle in his hand. As he watched, the stick straightened and turned blue, then red, and finally gold.

Eric shivered. "Oh, no . . . it can't be . . ."

Finally, a purple flower pushed itself out of the far end of the stick. The petals began to glow.

"The wand of Urik!" he whispered.

Even as he trembled holding it, Eric felt the power of the wand running through him.

"We did find it," he murmured. "And I kept trying to throw you away — I can't believe it. This is amazing. It's awesome. We actually did it. We found the wand!"

Eric suddenly remembered everything that Galen had done with the wand. But more than that, it was this wand — this same wand! — that created the rainbow staircase itself!

He stared at it. "Your magic can do *any-thing*!"

Without thinking twice, Eric ran down-stairs.

He flung open his front door.

Clutching the wand firmly in his hand, he marched right across the street.

To Julie's house.

About the Author

Tony Abbott is the author of more than three dozen funny novels for young readers, including the popular *Danger Guys* books and *The Weird Zone* series. Since childhood he has been drawn to stories that challenge the imagination, and, like Eric, Julie, and Neal, he often dreamed of finding doors that open to other worlds. Now that he is older — though not quite as old as Galen Longbeard — he believes he may have found some of those doors. They are called books. Tony Abbott was born in Ohio and now lives with his wife and two daughters in Connecticut.

For more information about Tony Abbott and the continuing saga of Droon, visit *www.tonyabbottbooks.com*.

THE SECRETS OF DROON

A Magical Series by Tony Abbott

Under the stairs, a magical world awaits you!

- ❏ BDK 0-590-10839-5   **#1: The Hidden Stairs and the Magic Carpet**
- ❏ BDK 0-590-10841-7   **#2: Journey to the Volcano Palace**
- ❏ BDK 0-590-10840-9   **#3: The Mysterious Island**
- ❏ BDK 0-590-10842-5   **#4: City in the Clouds**
- ❏ BDK 0-590-10843-3   **#5: The Great Ice Battle**
- ❏ BDK 0-590-10844-1   **#6: The Sleeping Giant of Goll**
- ❏ BDK 0-439-18297-2   **#7: Into the Land of the Lost**
- ❏ BDK 0-439-18298-0   **#8: The Golden Wasp**
- ❏ BDK 0-439-20772-X   **#9: The Tower of the Elf King**
- ❏ BDK 0-439-20784-3   **#10: Quest for the Queen**
- ❏ BDK 0-439-20785-1   **#11: The Hawk Bandits of Tarkoom**
- ❏ BDK 0-439-20786-X   **#12: Under the Serpent Sea**
- ❏ BDK 0-439-30606-X   **#13: The Mask of Maliban**
- ❏ BDK 0-439-30607-8   **#14: Voyage of the *Jaffa Wind***
- ❏ BDK 0-439-30608-6   **#15: The Moon Scroll**

$3.99 each!

Available Wherever You Buy Books or Use This Order Form

Scholastic Inc., P.O. Box 7502, Jefferson City, MO 65102

Please send me the books I have checked above. I am enclosing $_____ (please add $2.00 to cover shipping and handling). Send check or money order—no cash or C.O.D.s please.

Name_____Birth date_____

Address_____

City_____State/Zip_____

Please allow four to six weeks for delivery. Offer good in U.S.A. only. Sorry, mail orders are not available to residents of Canada. Prices subject to change.

www.scholastic.com

SCHOLASTIC   SD402